BADGER'S PARTY

For Max and Felix – H.O.
For Mum and Dad – S.V.

First published in Great Britain by Andersen Press in 1994.
First published in Picture Lions in 1996.

10 9 8 7 6

Picture Lions is an imprint of the Children's Division, part of
HarperCollins Publishers Ltd, 77-85 Fulham Palace Road, Hammersmith, London W6 8JB.

Printed and bound in Singapore. ISBN: 0 00 664554 2

BADGER'S PARTY

Story by Hiawyn Oram • Pictures by Susan Varley

PictureLions

An Imprint of HarperCollins*Publishers*

Badger was giving a party. Bat brought the invitations.

"Oh, do look," said Fieldmouse, reading hers. "It's a Bring-Something Party."

"A Bring-Something Party!" said Hedgehog. "What a good idea."

"I'll take fairycakes," said Squirrel. "I'm good at those."

"I'll take elderberry juice," said Stoat. "I've got crates."

Mole felt very grumpy. He didn't like the sound of a Bring-Something Party at all.

He went to find Badger.

 "Thanks for the invitation," he said, "but I won't be able to come. I haven't got anything to bring and I'm too busy building my new house to make anything."

"Oh dear," said Badger. "Hmm. Oh dear, oh hmm. Well, I suppose you could just bring yourself."

"Just myself?" said Mole.

"Yes," said Badger. "I mean, everyone else will be bringing something, but yes...umm, er...if you don't mind, just bring yourself."

So Mole went to the party without anything, just himself. His muddy, unwashed, unslicked-down self, not at all smart or dressed up.

Everyone else was in their party best. Everyone else had brought all sorts of lovely things.

Owl had brought streamers. Rat had brought funny hats. Squirrel had brought her fairycakes and Stoat his elderberry juice. Snail had brought her beautiful young daughter.

Fieldmouse had brought
her beautiful young son. Frog
had brought flowers, Weasel had brought
balloons. Hedgehog had brought honey sandwiches,
Rabbit had brought some old dance steps her mother
had taught her and Bat had brought his accordion.

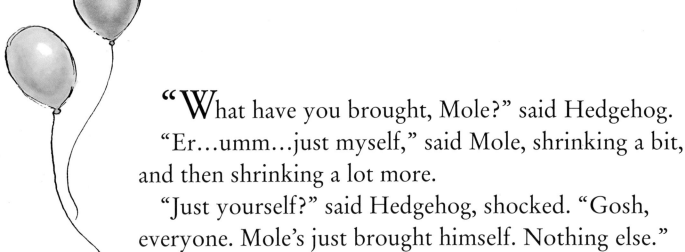

"What have you brought, Mole?" said Hedgehog.

"Er…umm…just myself," said Mole, shrinking a bit, and then shrinking a lot more.

"Just yourself?" said Hedgehog, shocked. "Gosh, everyone. Mole's just brought himself. Nothing else."

"Just himself," said Rabbit. "Well, I never did! And to think we've all brought ourselves AND something else."

"Exactly," said Fieldmouse.

"It's not fair," said Weasel. "We could all have not bothered and just brought ourselves and nothing else."

"Exactly," said all the others.

Mole felt about one centimetre high.

How he wished and wished and wished he'd thought of something to bring. Anything at all. Even that half–full bottle of sauce he had in his larder. (Someone might have enjoyed it in a sandwich.) Even that old whizz-banger thing he'd got last New Year's Eve. (Someone might have enjoyed whizzing it.)

He crept into a corner and ate a fairycake and had a glass of elderberry juice, feeling quite, quite awful. In fact, feeling quite certain that everyone at the party was pointing and saying, "Look, there's the One Who Didn't Bring Anything To A Bring-Something Party Except His Muddy Self."

And he was right. That's exactly what everyone was saying.

Beautiful Miss Snail was dancing with beautiful Master Fieldmouse. It was slow, so there was lots of time to talk.

"Oh, do look," said Miss Snail. "There's Mole. The One Who Didn't Bring Anything To A Bring-Something Party."

"Except His Muddy Self," said Squirrel, dancing past with Stoat, her nose stuck in the air.

"I hope you feel awful," said Rat, strolling over, "and by the way, I'm not giving you a funny hat because you're a Bring-Something Party pooper."

"OK," said Mole. "I won't have a funny hat. And yes, I do feel awful."

He took another slurp of elderberry juice and a bite of fairycake and since Stoat and Squirrel had brought them he felt even worse.

Then Badger sidled up.

"Look, old chap," he said. "I know I said it was all right not to bring anything but yourself, but I didn't mean your miserable, stand-in-a-corner-and-feel-sorry-for-yourself self. I meant your usual self. Your INTERESTING self."

A light flashed in Mole's head.

"Oh, THAT self," said Mole.

The light flashed again.

"Then everything's all right. Because, as it happens, I did bring my interesting self. I've got it right here."

"Hi, Frog," he said, stepping in an interesting way out of his corner.

"Hi, Molie," said Frog. "Howyadoin'?"

"Good," said Mole. "I'm doin' good. Seen any interesting dance steps lately, Frog?"

"Only the ones Rabbit brought," said Frog.

"Then check out THESE!" said Mole, who hadn't had a single dance step in his head until that moment. But now he invented a whole dance full.

"Wow, those are some dance steps," said Rat.
"They're incredible. Go slow, Mole, and show me!"
Mole showed him. Soon the whole party was
doing Mole's interesting dance steps.

"This is the best fun ever!" they all said, before they got tired and stopped for more elderberry juice and fairycakes.

"Anyone seen any interesting party tricks lately?" said Mole during the lull.

"Nope," everyone said, looking round.

"Well, look at this," said Mole. He put some streamers up his sleeve and pulled them out of a funny hat.

"Wow!" said everyone. "That's a great trick, Molie!"

Then he asked the beautiful
Miss Snail if she'd perch on a
fairycake. He put the fairycake
on top of a bottle of elderberry
juice and he balanced the whole
lot on his snout, before it fell off.

Miss Snail landed softly and
everyone was terribly entertained.
They clapped and laughed and
shouted, "More! More!"

Badger was very pleased. Mole had brought
something really special to his Bring-Something
Party: dance steps that had just been invented
and some very entertaining entertainment.

As Mole was leaving, Badger gave him a
big badger hug.

"Thanks for coming, Mole," he said.

"Thanks for inviting me," said Mole.

"It was a great party."

And it must have been because the next day it was the talk of the woods.

"Well, as it was such a success," said Badger, "I'd better give another one next week."

"I'll bring the fairycakes," said Squirrel.

"I'll bring my accordion," said Bat.

"I'll bring half a bottle of sauce and a whizz-banger," said Mole.

"And yourself, I hope," said Fieldmouse anxiously.

"And your dance steps and party tricks," said everyone, anxiously.

"Of course," said Mole, burrowing into his new foundations and thinking how deep-down good it felt to have so much to bring to Badger's next Bring-Something Party.

Here are some more Picture Lions

BADGER'S PARTING GIFTS
Susan Varley

Quentin Blake
MISTER MAGNOLIA

KATIE MORAG AND THE TIRESOME TED
Mairi Hedderwick

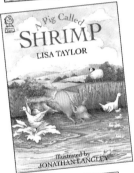

A Pig Called SHRIMP
LISA TAYLOR
Illustrated by JONATHAN LANGLEY

A BAD WEEK FOR The Great
TONY BRADMAN & JENNY WILLIAMS

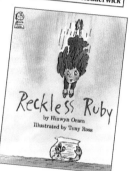

Reckless Ruby
by Hiawyn Oram
Illustrated by Tony Ross

Monsters
Colin & Jacqui Hawkins

WHERE THE WILD THINGS ARE
STORY AND PICTURES BY MAURICE SENDAK

SNOWY

for you to enjoy